This **Chicken House** book belongs to
....
That's **Me!**

For Poppie, Louis, Imogen and Isaac
– each of you a delight.
With love from Auntie Sara.
– S. S.

For all my favourite Sarahs
– M. C.

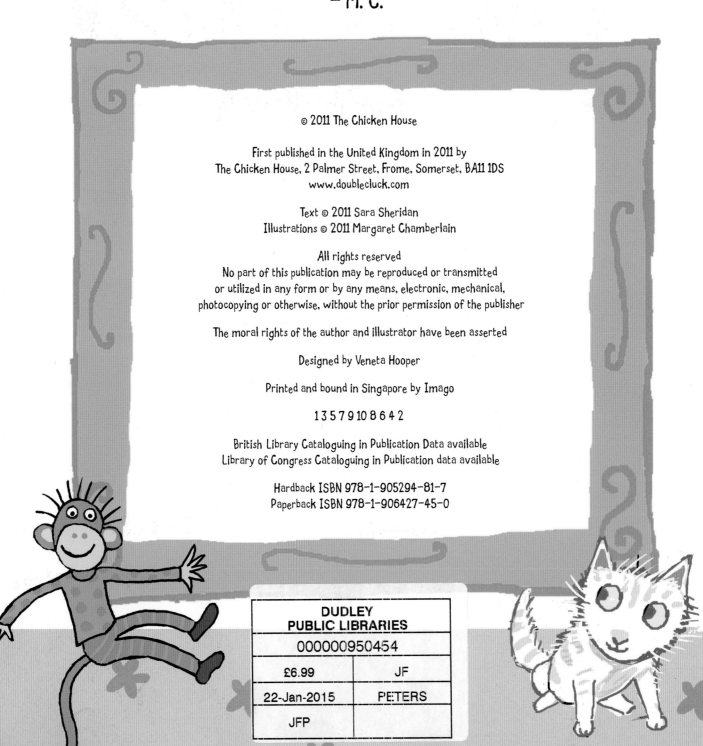

© 2011 The Chicken House

First published in the United Kingdom in 2011 by
The Chicken House, 2 Palmer Street, Frome, Somerset, BA11 1DS
www.doublecluck.com

Text © 2011 Sara Sheridan
Illustrations © 2011 Margaret Chamberlain

Designed by Veneta Hooper

Printed and bound in Singapore by Imago

1 3 5 7 9 10 8 6 4 2

British Library Cataloguing in Publication Data available
Library of Congress Cataloguing in Publication data available

Hardback ISBN 978-1-905294-81-7
Paperback ISBN 978-1-906427-45-0

Who wants to be a princess, a pirate, or a knight?

I'm Me!

Sara Sheridan

Illustrated by

Margaret Chamberlain

Chicken House

'Hello Auntie Sara, it's me!'

'Hello you!
What shall we play today?

Will you be . . .

...a naughty monkey?'
suggested Auntie Sara.

'And I'm feeding you **fruit** on a **hot** sandy beach, and we're watching the **dolphins** and **sharks!**'

'Hmmm, not today,' said Imogen.

'Today I want to be . . .'

'. . . a beautiful princess?' said Auntie Sara. 'And we're riding white horses and dancing all night, under the twinkling sky!'

'Hmmm,
not today,'
said Imogen.

'Today I want
to be ...'

'. . . . a witch's cat?' said Auntie Sara.

'And we're **whizzing** along on my broomstick so fast, casting our powerful spells!'

'Hmmm, not today,' said Imogen.

'Today I want to be . . .'

'. . . a pirate's parrot?' said Auntie Sara.

'And we're plundering treasure from ships on the sea, being fearsome and fearless and gruff!'

'Hmmm, not today,' said Imogen.

'Today I want to be . . .'

'. . . a dragon-taming knight?'
said Auntie Sara. And we're teaching our dragons to
loop the **loop** through **hoops** and fly **high** in the sky!'

...an adventurous astronaut?'

said Auntie Sara. 'And we're zooming through space, passing planets and stars, looking for aliens on Mars!

'Hmmm,
not today,'
said Imogen.

'Today I just
want to be . . .'

. . . Me!'

'Oh!' said Auntie Sara. 'And what would **you** like to do today?'

'Follow me!' said Imogen. 'We'll . . .

. . . go to the **park**.

And we'll **play** on the **swings** and **sing** out **loud** until we're out of **puff** and go **pink!**

'And then **we'll . . .**

...eat **ice cream**,' said Imogen.

'Mmm...the **stickiest, drippiest, yummiest** cones, the **biggest** we've **ever seen!**'

'And then
we'll . . .

... **go back home.** And we'll snuggle up tight for some stories about **witches** and **dragons** and **knights!**

Today, Auntie, what I want is for **you** to be **you** and **me** to be **Me!**'

And Auntie Sara agreed.